몸의 사원

이정미 시집

Dancing Every-Body

Jungmi Lee

English translation ChatGPT

이정미

철학을 전공한 예술치료사.
몸과 움직임을 탐색하는 무용/동작심리치료사.
미국 IMS (Integrated Movemnt Studies)에서 라반/바르테니
에프 동작분석 (Laban/Bartenieff Movement Analysis) 자격
을 취득하였고 현재 병원에서 발달장애인들과 작업하고 있다.

몸의 사원

Dancing Every-Body

이정미 시집

Jungmi Lee

목 차

1부 몸
BODY

이미 거기 있다

내 하얀 뼈들은 이미 거기 있다

만져보려 느껴보려 해도 알 수 없던
뼈의 자리와 뼈들의 속삭임들
어느 성소의 만트라처럼
진흙을 품은 연꽃처럼

무딘 감각과 분주한 생각들로
미처 알아차리지 못했을 뿐이다
내가 알지 못하는 한없이 가뿐한 내가
무거운 나를 이끌고 걸어간다

요란한 아우성이
멀리 어렴풋이 들리는 찬미 소리를 덮고
텅 빈 공간을 가로 지른다

엄마가 우는 아기를 품듯이
아우성을 보듬는
여백의 마음
내 하얀 뼈들이 이미 거기 있다

Already there

My white bones are already there

Even if I try to touch them or feel them,
I can't sense the bones' positions or their whispers
Like a mantra of a certain shrine
Like the withered flowers holding mud

It's just that my dull senses and hurried thoughts
Couldn't figure it out in time
My ignorance and carefree self
Leads me, carrying this heavy burden

The wild roar
Covering the sounds of praise that can be heard from far
away
Pierces through the empty space

Like a mother holding her crying baby
The emptiness of mind comforts the roar
My white bones are already there

다시 (दासी) (Yield)

20대 초반, 나에겐 한없이 의뭉스러운 인도의 성자에게
'다시(दासी)'라는 제자명을 받은 여자를 만났다

언니, '다시' 뜻이 뭐야?
산스크리트어로 하녀야
yield하라고, Surrender하라고
'승리하다'가 아니고 '항복하다'라니
검은색 양장 영한사전을 펼치고
나는 이상한 이름이라고 생각했다

강변 2층집 세 얻은 작은 방에서
정원으로 이어진 창문으로
길게 걸쳐진 그림자를 보며
'하녀' 같은 이름을 지어주는
인도 성자의 제자는 되고 싶지 않다고 생각했다
밀어붙이고 달려 나가 움켜 당겨오고 싶었던 시기였다

억새가 무성한 강둑으로 나가면
발등까지 차오른 검은 진흙에서 축축한 흙냄새가 났다
발의 기억이 시간을 건너 말한다, '다시'

Dasi (दासी) (Yield)

In my early 20s, I met a woman
who went by the name "Dasi" given to her by an vague Indian
guru
"Sister, what does 'Dasi' mean?"
"It means maid in Sanskrit."
It means to yield, to surrender
It's not about victory, it's about submission,
I looked it up in my black leather English-Korean
dictionary
and thought the name was strange

I lay on the small room on the second floor of a riverside
apartment
gazing out the window that led to the garden.
Looking at the long shadows that stretched out,
I didn't want to be a disciple of an Indian guru
who gave me a name like a maid
I wanted to push away, to run out and pull back

When I went riverside where the silver grass in lush
I could smell the damp earth in the thick black mud
that reached up to my ankles
The memory of my feet talks across time, "Dasi."

연애 지침 (Grap)

손을 먼저 잡으세요
긴장을 풀어요
흥건해진 손바닥에선 미끄러지기 쉬워요
레고처럼 손바닥의 아귀를 맞춰요
처음부터 마치 하나였던 것처럼 느껴요

나를 그에게 녹여요
나를 담은 살갗을 넓게 도려내어
연서를 쓰세요
나는 왜 네가 아닌가 애통해하며
당신을 먹을 만큼 사랑한다고

콩알이 껍질을 벗기고 뿌리를 내리듯이
한 개의 콩알이 두 쪽의 떡잎이 되듯
나뉘지 않은 것이 둘이 되는 것
그것이 땅의 일임을 고백하세요

시간을 거슬러 사랑하세요
움켜쥔 손을 놓고
이미 나뉘지 않는 하나였음을
그것이 하늘의 일임을 속삭이세요

Guidelines on Love (Grap)

Hold hands first
Let go of tension
It's easy to slip on sweaty palms
Fit the curves of your hands like Lego
Feel like you were one from the beginning

Melt me into him
Write a love letter with the flesh that holds me
questioning why I'm me and not you, tormented
you love him enough to eat him up

Like a bean sprout shedding its shell and rooting down
One bean becomes two sprouts
Confess that it's the work of the earth
To turn one into two

Love across time
Let go of clasped hands
We are already one indivisible entity
Whisper that it's the work of the sky

봄비를 맞이하는 꽃의 자세 (Yield)

만화경의 꽃들이 피고 지는 동안
꽃잎이 파르르 꽃샘추위에 떤다
사라지고 다시 태어나는 것들에게 입 맞추리
한차례 몸살처럼 뒤흔들자
우수수 바람 따라 흩날린다
오라! 오라! 몇 번이고 다시 오라!

Embracing Spring Rain (Yield)

While the flowers of the kaleidoscope bloom and wither,
The petals fall in the chilly breath of spring,
I kiss them, those who disappear and are born again,
Like a bout of illness, shaking the branches
Fluttering in the wind, they scatter and disperse,
Come, come on, again and again!

목걸이 (Breathe)

한 호흡으로
파란 팬던트가 천돌에 고인다
나는 아주 오랫동안 반도네온처럼
늑간근을 펼쳤다 오무리며
짚시의 노래로 흐느꼈다
영화를 잃어버린 옛 성터처럼
흉곽은 바람이 나갈 곳을 찾지 못했다
잃어버린 사랑인 줄 알았다

흐르는 눈물이 불러오는
따뜻한 오후의 시에스타
이 모든 것이 어디서 왔느냐
이 먼 곳까지 흘러온 한 줌 빛
욥이 사기로 긁어낸 부스럼 밑 붉은 피부처럼
쓰라리면서 기쁘다
잠든 동안에도 심장이 뛰고
폐가 물가에서 속닥인다

사랑한다고 사랑한다고

Necklace (Breathe)

With one breath,
The blue pendant settles on the rock.
I had stretched out my chest for a long time
Like a neon sign, sighing with tears.
Like an old castle lost in prosperity and glory
My chest couldn't find a place for the wind to escape.
I thought it was a lost love.

Under the warm afternoon siesta
summoned by flowing tears,
Where did all this come from?
A handful of light that flowed all the way here,
Like the reddish skin under Job's scraped scabs,
It hurts but it's happy.
Even while asleep, the heart beats
And the lungs whisper in the water.

I love you, I love you.

정월대보름 (세포호흡)

달이 그득 차고 온 세상이 환하다
나랏님은 언제나
백성의 마음이 천심이라 했다

지역마다 고을마다
보릿고개 하루하루
백성들이 잘 먹고 살고 있는지
알뜰히 살피지 못하면
참다참다 성난 민심
떠받들던 옥좌를 내려놓고
봉기의 열기가 꽃처럼 번진다

내 몸 곳곳
오장육부 굽이굽이
세포 하나하나
숨 쉬며 쏟아내는 소리를 알아차리지 못하면
나랏님 궁궐도 허사인 줄 알면서도
거기에 온 마음이 깃든 줄 알면서도
그동안 못 들은 소식

아침 일찍 이명주(耳明酒)*한 잔

아둔한 귀를 밝혀

즐거운 소식을 듣자꾸나

---

* 이명주: 정월 대보름날 아침 식전에 마시면 귀가 밝아진다는 술. 귀밝이술을 마시
면 일 년 동안 귀가 밝아지고 좋은 소식을 듣게 된다고 믿었다.

On the night of the first full moon
(Cellular respiration)

The moon is full and the whole world is bright

The king always said

The hearts of the people are like the heavens

In each region, in each village

over the time of famine, day by day,

If he cannot carefully inspect

whether the people are well- fed and living well

Enduring, enduring, the public's rage

Laying down the jade throne they once held high

The heat of the uprising spreads like blooming flowers

Every part of my body

Every crevice and every fold

Each and every cell

Breathes and emits a sound If we don't realize this

Even if we know that the royal palace is just an empty
shell

Even if our hearts are tied to it

We have been unaware of good news

So let us drink a glass of ear-opening wine*

On this morning

To clear our dull ears

And hear some joyful news

---

* Ear opening wine is a Korean traditional liquor that is believed to brighten
one's hearing. It is traditionally consumed in the morning of the first full moon
day of the lunar new year, and it is believed that drinking it will improve one's
hearing and bring good news throughout the year.

중심잡기 (Centering)

One, Two, Three 한쪽 다리를 들고 균형을 잡아 봐요
One, Two, Three 발은 순례자처럼 절실히 땅에 입 맞추고요
One, Two, Three 발가락은 텐트를 고정하는 핀처럼 땅에 박
아두세요
One, Two, Three 휘파람을 불며 자유로워진 다리로 허공에
원을 그려봐요
One, Two, Three 향로를 든 수도승처럼 미끄러지듯 중심을
옮겨 봐요

변덕의 마음을 죽 끓이듯
이리저리 휘젓는 주걱처럼
골반을 이고 길게 뻗은 두 다리로
번갈아 땅을 디디며 생각해요

이 마음과 저 마음 다 들만 했지
유명한 약사가 약을 조제하듯
One, Two, Three 변덕의 두 팔 저울에
고갱이의 추를 올려봐요

Centering

One, two, three, lift one leg and find balance

One, two, three, press your feet onto the ground like a pilgrim

One, two, three, anchor your toes into the earth like a tent peg

One, two, three, whistle and draw circles in the air with a free leg

One, two, three, Try shifting your weight like a monk holding a censer

Stirring the fickle heart as if boiling soup

Like a ladle swinging back and forth

With the pelvis carrying the long extended legs

Alternately stepping on the ground, I ponder

It's only natural this thought and that thought kept coming to mind

Like a famous pharmacist preparing medicine

One, two, three, try placing the weight of core

On the scale of whimsical arms

너에게 나를 당겨오다 (Pull)

그의 손을 잡기 전엔 알지 못했다
단단히 움켜잡은 팔의 힘으로
그에게 매달리듯 다가가는 방법밖에는

그래서 사랑이 항상 어긋났구나
다가가고자 애쓰는 나의 무게를
감당해 줄 사람이 필요하다고 생각했다

그는 단단히 서서 부드러운 팔을 내밀며 말했다
중심을 가져오라고
제자가 스승 옆에 앉아 배움을 시작하듯
매달리지 않고 중심을 옮기는 법
너에게 나를 당겨온다

Pulling myself towards You (Pull)

Before I held his hand, I didn't know
that I only knew how to approach someone
by clinging with the strength of tightly gripped arms

So love has always been misaligned
I thought I needed someone to bear
the weight of my efforts to get closer

Standing firm, he extended his soft arms and said
"Bring your center"
Like a disciple sitting next to a master to learn
not clinging, but shifting the center
Pulling myself towards you

저절로 일어나는 일

나한테 호흡을 맡기지 않아서 다행이야
아마 그랬더라면
푸른 얼굴을 갖게 되었을 거야
이토록 바쁜 세상에
1분에 몇 십 번
숨을 할딱거리는 것까지
그것까지 내가 해야 하는 일이었다면
위태로운 임시정부의 채권처럼
길바닥을 쓸며 나뒹굴고 있을지도 몰라
저절로 일어나는 일들
그 일에 집중하기만 하면 더 잘 일어나는 일이
나에게도 있다니

나한테 심장을 맡기지 않아서 다행이야
아마 그랬더라면
쥐락펴락 심장을 조여야 했겠지
이토록 쉴 없는 세상에
1분에 몇 십 번
심장을 펌핑하는 것까지

그것까지 내가 해야 하는 일이였다면
악덕업주가 이주노동자의 임금을 체불하듯
빈혈(貧血)을 피할 수 없었겠지
심장이 터져라 모터를 돌리며
피들이 솟구치도록 함성을 지르는
그런 파이팅 넘치는 일들이
나에게도 저절로 일어난다니

Things that happen naturally

I'm glad I don't have to rely on myself for breathing
Otherwise,
I might have turned blue
In such a busy world
If I had to take every breath
every few seconds
I might be sweeping the streets and crawling around
Like the precarious bonds of a provisional governmen
There are things that happen naturally
And I've realized that
I do better when I focus on them

I'm glad I don't have to rely on myself for my heartbeat
Otherwise,
I might have been squeezing my throbbing heart
In such an unrelenting world
If I had to pump my heart every few seconds
I might have suffered from anemia
like an evil employer withholding an immigrant's salary

But there are things that happen naturally

And I've found that I can also tackle those high-spirited tasks,

With my heart pumping like a roaring engine

And my blood boiling like an excited cheer

날숨

숨을 잡고 있었다
삶의 광폭함을 견디기 위해
비행을 지켜줄 안전한 낙하산처럼
가슴 한 웅큼 쥐고 있었다
머리카락이 잔뜩 엉킨
수챗구멍을 빠져나가는 물처럼
끽끽 소리를 내며
간신히 내쉬고 있었다
이제 놓아도 돼
지면에 닿은 신체를 느끼며
비행이 아님을
낙하가 아님을

낮은 지형으로 물이 흘러가듯
세상의 끝인 이과수 폭포처럼
일제히 하강한다
남은 숨들이 매듭을 푼다
이제 놓아도 돼

Exhalation

I was holding my breath,
Like a reliable parachute
to withstand the vastness of life
I was clutching it in my chest
Like water escaping through a tangled hole
of disheveled hair
I gasped for air
with a wheezing sound
Barely managing to exhale
Now I can let go
Feeling my body touch the ground
Realizing it's not flying
It's not falling

Like water flowing down a low terrain,
We descend together like
the end of the world, the Igwazu Falls
Our remaining breaths are released
Now I can let go

부드러운 척추

부산 앞바다 포장마차에서
징그러워 접시 가장자리로 밀어 둔 개불
심플이즈베스트가 모토이지만
삶은 언제나 염려로 가득 찼다

징그러움은 익숙하지 않은 것들을 느끼는 방식일 뿐
소주 한 잔 털어 넣고
개불 한 점 먹으면서
시작에서 끝으로 가는 도중
차르르 흔들림을 헤아린다

입과 똥구멍 라인의 변화무쌍한 디자인들이
삼삼오오 잔을 털고 있다

Soft Spine

At the food cart near Busan's sea
feeling unpleasant I pushed penis fish to the edge of the
plate
Simplicity is the best
but my life was always full of worries

Disgust is just a way of experiencing unfamiliar things
While drinking a shot of soju
and eating a piece of penis fish
I calculate the shudder that goes from start to end.

Various designs of changes in the mouth and anus line
In groups of three and five, emptying their cups

ㄱ (Head-Tail)

간난시절 할머니 등에 업혀 세상을 맡아서인지
나는 그녀의 홀쭉해진 가슴팍을 좋아했다
젊어서는 그렇지 않았는데 왜 이리 눈이 쬐끄매지냐
하시며 닦아내던 진물 많던 눈도
너는 낭군이 그리 좋냐며 헛웃음 짓던 수줍은 입도
양념치킨을 사 갈 때마다
이런 건 처음 먹어본다 하시던 목소리도
손녀 오기 전부터 엿질금과 고두밥을 식혜로 삭히고
막걸리 빵을 부풀려 찜통에서 꺼내주시던
그 쭈글쭈글한 손도 좋아했다

일찍부터 무릎에 귀를 걸어둘 고리를 찾으신 듯
허리가 ㄱ자로 꺽여서 땅만 보고 걸으셨다
허리도 똑바로 세우고 걸을 수 없는 당신이 너무 부끄러워
사람 다니지 않는 한적한 뒷골목으로 비탈을 내려가셨다

그 등에 자식들이 업히고
12명의 손자 손녀들이 업히고
가난이 업히고

남편 잡아먹은 한이 업히고

똑바로 세울 수 없었던 그녀의 허리
그 허리 하나하나
나의 골반 위에 가지런히 얹어
그리움의 탑돌이를 하고 싶다

ㄱ* (Head-Tail)

I, who smelled the world on my grandmother's back

when I was a baby, came to love her slender chest

she said, "I wasn't like this when I was young,

why do my eyes become narrow now?"

I loved her tearful eyes she often wiping away

Even her shy smile, asking if I liked husband, was

endearing

And her voice saying "This is the first time I've tried this."

whenever buying seasoned fried chicken,

I loved her wrinkled hands

that soaked barley candies and millet in sweet rice drink

and took the makgeolli bread out from the steamer

It seemed like she had been searching for a loop

to hang her ear on her knee,

Her back bent in a 'ㄱ' shape,

eyes always on the ground when she walked.

---

* ㄱ is the first korean alphabet.

Embarrassed that she couldn't stand up straight,
she would walk down a deserted alley on a hillside.

Her back carried her children,
12 grandchildren,
Poverty,
Carrying the resentment of a wife who devoured her
husband

I want to carefully place her curved waist,
One by one, onto my own hips,
And I want to do the spinning around the pagoda of
yearning.

미어캣에게 보내는 편지 (감각하는 머리와 꼬리)

얼마 전 동물원에서 너희들을 봤어
굴에서 나와 허리를 곧추세우고
파수꾼처럼 서 있는 너희들을 말야

두리번거리는 눈이
사막을 닮은 금빛 몸을 이끌고
긴장된 목과 어깨로 뾰족하게 서있더라
전쟁을 모르는 것들은
두려움도 없다고
혀를 차면서

붉은 눈을 덮은 파르르 떨리는 눈꺼풀
나도 너희 엄마를 닮은 것 같구나
두려움 많은 것들만이 공격하지

해 질 무렵
뜨뜻한 사막 위에
소화되지 않은 아랫배를 깔고 엎드려서
노을을 한참 보고 싶구나

입을 살짝 벌리고
해가 사라지는 방향으로 고개를 돌리며
엉덩이가 씰룩거리는 것을 느끼고 싶구나

하얀 깃발을 들고 서 있을께
피크닉 날을 알려줘

Dear Meerkat (Head and Tail)

I saw you and your family at the zoo not long ago
Emerging from your burrow, standing tall and vigilant
like sentries

Your restless eyes led your golden body resembling the
desert
Standing sharp with tense neck and shoulders
click their tongues, saying that
Those who know not of war
there's no fear either

trembling eyelids covered with red eyes
And I think I take after her
Only those who fear attack

As the sun sets
I want to lie down on the heated sand
Spread out my undigested organs

And watch the sunset for a long time
I want to slightly open my mouth
Turn my head towards the direction where the sun
disappears
And feel my buttocks wriggle

I'll stand with a white flag
Let me know when it's picnic day

순심 (Tail)

순심이가 경련으로 쓰러진 뒤
한 달 만에 집에 돌아왔지만
걷지도 음식을 먹지도 못했다
주사기로 죽을 입에 흘려 넣어주고
자기 똥을 밟은 젤리 같은 발바닥을 닦아주고
그냥 살아있기만을 바랐다
그랬던 그이가 다시 출입문에 서서
꼬리를 흔들며 우리를 환영한다

어떤 이는 부모를 그리 모시라 했고
어떤 이는 자연스럽게 순리를 따르는 것이 좋다 했다
하지만 어쩌랴
모든 사랑은 작고 어린 것으로 흐르고
모든 기쁨은 척추를 타고 흐른다

환영과 기쁨의 선생님, 순심

Soonshim, my dog (Tail)

After Soonshim collapsed from seizures
It took a month for her to come back home
But she couldn't walk or eat
We injected her with medicine and fed it to her dying
mouth
Wiped her jelly-like feet that had stepped on her own
poop
And just hoped she would stay alive
But there she was again, standing at the entrance
Wagging her tail to welcome us

Some say to honor their parents
While others say to follow the natural order
But what can we do?
All love flows through small and young things
And all joy flows through our spines

Welcome and joy's teacher, Soonshim.

반쪽이 (Body half)

전래동화 반쪽이*는
눈 하나, 귀 하나, 팔 하나
예쁜 색시를 찾아
재주 한 번 넘고는
미남자가 되었단다

두 개의 가지를 뻗은 한 몸
너는 마치 내가 미처 가보지 못한 길처럼
나를 꿈꾸게 한다

어눌한 한 쪽이 코를 들이마시며
머뭇거리는 폼이 영 시원찮아도
뭉툭한 그 다리가 땅을 디뎌줄 때
영특한 반쪽이도 신바람 타고 다리를 치켜든다

─────────────

* 반쪽이 설화: 반쪽의 몸을 지닌 주인공이 과업을 달성하여 잘산다고 하는 내용의
설화

Body half

In the folk tale, Body half*
One eye, one ear, one arm
Looking for a pretty bride
And with a single rotation
He become a beautiful man

With two branches stretched out in one body
You, like a path I have yet to explore
Inspire me to dream

Even though one side hesitates, sniffing in a nasal tone,
And the form might not seem too appealing
When that blunt leg steps on the ground
That unique other half lifts its leg and feels invigorated

---

* Body Half folktale: A story of a protagonist with half of his body who achieves
success and becomes wealthy.

무릎

땅을 딛고 설 수 없을 때
무릎으로라도 서고 싶었지
그래서 내 무릎은
거북이 등딱지처럼
딱딱하게 굳었어
한 번도 넘어진 적 없는
매끈한 무릎이고 싶었는데

정원 옆 수돗가에서
깨알처럼 박힌 모래알들과
피범벅 된 무릎을 씻어내고 있었지
모래를 되새김하는 조개에게
진주의 가치란 더 이상 따갑지 않다는 거야

허영과 교만한 마음을 작게 접으려 할 때
딱딱한 무릎을 꿇고 손을 모은다
얼마나 잘 넘어지는 너였느냐
연약한 것들을 단단하게 하는 무릎이란
어느 순간 나를 잘 접을 수 있는 경첩 같은 것

Knees

When I cannot stand on the ground
I wanted to stand on my knees
So my knees became
As hard as a turtle's shell.
I wanted smooth knees
That had never fallen before

Next to the garden by the faucet,
I washed off the sand, tiny as sesame seeds
And my blood-stained knees
To a clam that grinds sand
The value of a pearl is no longer being sharp

When I try to fold my vanity and arrogance small
I kneel on these hard knees and clasp my hands
How well you used to fall
Knees that make fragile things strong
Like a hinge that can fold me well at any moment

둥글게 둥글게

내 손가락과 너의 손가락이
내 팔이 너의 목덜미에
내 뺨이 너의 뺨에 둥글게 닿아있다
순례자들이 손을 맞추고
원을 그리며 춤을 추듯
나는 너에게
가장 둥근 가슴을 내어준다
작고 귀여운 아가야
우리가 이렇게 둥글게
맞닿을 수 있어 은혜롭다
나의 피는 젖이 되어 너에게 흐르리
너의 입천장에서 분수처럼 분사되어 목을 축이리
쒸익쒸익 맹렬한 욕망의 쇠된 소리
삼킴에는 언제나 리듬이 필요하다

아가의 봉긋한 이마에
송글송글 땀이 맺힌다

Round and round

My fingers and yours,

my arm around your neck,

my cheek pressed against yours, round and round.

Like pilgrims joining hands

dancing in a circle

I offer you the roundest of hearts

Oh small and lovely one,

how gracious that we can meet

round and round.

My blood will turn to milk for you,

fountain-like, spewing from your lips

throttling your throat with a rhythmic gulp

The creaking sound of fierce desires

A rhythm is always needed for swallowing

On the baby's high forehead

pearly beads of sweat form

중력(Heavy)

지구가

나를 끌어당겨

서 있을 힘도 없는걸

한 발짝도 더는 앞으로 못 딛겠어

꺼지는 땅으로 침몰하기 전에 구조 요청해야지

들리니 땅으로 빨려 들어가 좁아진 성대를 따라 가늘게 뱉어진 숨소리가

보이니 피사의 탑 같이 기울어진 어깨와 미미하게 흔들리는 두 팔의 포물선이

일어서지 못할 것을 두려워하지 마 대지에 몸을 맡기고 잠시 쉬어가도 괜찮아

Gravity (Heavy)

The Earth

is pulling me

I have no strength to stand

I can't take another step forward

Before sinking into the fading land, I should request rescue

Can you see the shoulders leaning like the Tower of Pisa and the arms trembling slightly in an arc?

Can you hear the thin breath being exhaled through the constricted vocal cords sucked into the ground

Don't be afraid of not being able to stand up it's okay to entrust your body to the earth and take a short rest

무게중심 옮기기

내가 알고 있는 결혼 만해도 세 번이지만
그가 몇 명의 부인과 애인이 있었는지 알지 못한다
그는 짧은 영어에 맛깔나게 유머를 무치고
쿠웨이트 사막에 길을 만들던 중년을 지나
필리핀 여자에게 새 장가를 들고
코로나 한창이던 봄날
카톡으로 숙박사업 소식을 전한다
오빠, 임자 만났나 보네
그 떠도는 마음이 닻을 내린 걸 보니
그가 웃는 얼굴의 오리 이모티콘을 보내며
난 언제나 임자를 만났었지 한다

사랑은 움직이고 그는 온 몸을 옮겼던 게지
엉덩이를 쭉 뺀 채 밍기적거리지 않고
손만 뻗어 사랑의 시늉을 하지는 않았던 게지
가장 밑바닥에 자신을 맡기고
감정이 움직이지 않으면 거칠게 밀어부쳤던 게지
언제나 임자를 만났던 게지

Weight shifing

I know that getting married three times is not enough
But I don't know how many wives and lovers he had
He passed through his middle age making jests with wit
in short English
And on a spring day during the peak of the corona virus
pandemic
He got a new bride from the Philippines
and sent news of his lodging business via Kakao talk
"Older brother, did you meet the right person?"
When I saw that his wandering heart had settled down
He sent me a smiling duck emoji on Kakao talk
And say I always have met the right person

Love moves, and he moved his whole body without
wiggling his hips never tried to show the gestures of love
with just his hand extended
He entrusted himself to the bottom of the bottom
and pushed his emotions roughly if they didn't move
And he always has met the right person

* 에포트 (Effort)는 움직임의 에너지적 측면을 의미하는 라반이 만든 용어이다. 독일어의 'Antrieb'에서 어원을 찾을 수 있는데 인간의 내적충동이나 마음의 상태가 움직임으로 드러나는 것을 의미한다.

2부 에포트
EFFORT

파수꾼의 꿈 (Free flow)

손목을 조여 오던 시계를 풀고
어느 바닷속 물미역처럼
한나절을 그렇게 보내고 싶어
흐느적 흐느적 머리 풀듯이 긴장을 풀고

잊고 있었네
나도 이렇게 춤출 수 있다는 것을
어느 활화산 꿀렁꿀렁 토한 용암처럼
길 없는 들판을 질주하고 싶어
여름밤 폭죽처럼
이리저리 꿈틀거리고 싶어
펑펑 소리를 요란하게 내며
삐죽삐죽 발광하고 싶어
지버리쉬로 기도하며
난장 마음을

우두커니 지켜보고 싶어

The Sentinel's Dream (Free flow)

Untie the watch tightening my wrist
and spend a whole day like seaweed in the sea
Loosen the tension, like letting out a sigh
and I realize I had forgotten
that I too can dance like this
I want to speed across the trackless plain
like the boiling lava of a volcano
and squirm like fireworks on a summer night,
bursting with loud pops and flashing lights.
I want to pray in gibberish
My wild heart

I want to silently watch over it

눈뜨는 잔치 (Free flow)*

인당수의 물을 물끄러미 바라보았다
좀처럼 뛰어들 용기가 나지 않았다
사랑이라니

눈물이 얼굴을 타고 흘러내리듯
삶의 주물에서 무력하게 찍혀 나온 그가
눈을 뜨기를 바랐다
타르초(Tharchog)를 읽는 바람처럼
그가 나를 읽기를 바랐다
폐허처럼 흘러내린 그 몸의
귀 조각이 나를 듣기를 바랐다

오색 조각으로 뜯겨져
바람에 한없이 휘몰아쳤던
그 모든 기억들이 운명이다

---

* 심청전은 한국의 고전소설이자 판소리계 소설이다. 맹인인 아버지의 눈을 띄우기
위해 공양미 삼백 석에 인당수에 빠질 재물로 팔려가는 딸 심청에 관한 이야기이다.
판소리에서는 심청의 효심에 감동한 하늘의 명으로 용왕이 생명을 구해주고 황후가
되어 아버지를 찾는 맹인 잔치를 벌인다. 이 잔치에서 아버지뿐만 아니라 잔치에 온
맹인들과 산천초목까지 눈을 뜨게 된다.

이제 허둥거리지 않고 깃발을 휘날릴 테다

어느 목사가 심청전의 마지막 대목을 알려주었다
심청이를 만난 심봉사가 눈을 뜨자
산천초목이 눈을 뜨고
봉사 잔치에 오는 중인 봉사들도 눈을 뜨고
잔치에서 돌아간 봉사들도 눈을 뜨고
이 눈뜨는 잔치에서 모든 이들이 춤을 출 것이다
바지가 흘러내리는 줄도 모르고
신명나게 춤을 출 것이다

보이지 않던 것이 보이고
있던 것이 없어지고
없던 것이 나타나는 잔치
기쁨이 흘러넘치고
발을 구르며
쾌지나 소리가 흥청거리는

Festival of Awakening (Free flow)*

I stared at the water in silence
I didn't have the courage to jump in
After all, love

Tears rolling down my face like a stream,
He who was beaten down by life's hammer,
Hoped to open his eyes
Like a wind reading a Tharchog
He hoped to read me
The earlobe of that broken body, like a ruin,
Hoped to hear me

All those memories, torn apart into rainbow pieces,
Uncontrollably blown around by the wind,

---

* Simcheongjeon is a classic Korean novel and a pansori (traditional Korean narrative song) tale. It's about Simcheong, a daughter who is sold into slavery for three hundred sacks of rice in order to restore her blind father's sight. In the pansori version, Simcheong's devotion moves the heavens to save her life and she becomes a queen who holds a banquet for blind people, in order to find her father. At the banquet, not only her father but also all the blind guests and the nearby mountain plants and flowers regain their sight.

Fate brought them here
Now, I'll raise my flag without faltering

A pastor told me the last chapter of Sim Cheong
When blind father met Sim Cheong, he opened his eyes
The mountain wild flowers opened their eyes,
The incoming the blind to the banquet opened their eyes,
The blind who had left the banquet opened their eyes
On this waking feast, everyone will dance,
Without noticing their pants falling down,
They'll dance with joy overflowing,

where things unseen become visible,
Where things present disappear,
And where nonexistent things appear.
At this waking feast
Rolling their feet
and shouting with ecstasy

영산회상불보살 靈山會相佛菩薩 (Bound)*

구멍을 막고

가지런하게 호흡을 모아서

대나무 관을 관통한다

현을 누르고 뜯고

활로 긁고 내리쳐서

단정하게 마음을 조율한다

양심(兩心)의 가죽을 두드리고

소리와 소리 사이를 조심스럽게 걷는다

버선코처럼 부드러운 곡선 끝에 뾰족한 산을 얹듯

부드럽지만 명료하고

우아하면서도 군더더기 없다

영축산에서 법화경을 설하시는 부처의 말씀을

나는 눈으로 듣는다

귀로 합창한다

보살의 자비와 덕을

손가락으로 변주하며 찬양한다

---

* 15세기의 음악을 기록한 「악학궤범」에 따르면 영산회상은 영산회상불보살이란 불교가사를 관현악 반주로 노래하던 불교음악이였으나 현대에 이르러서는 세속화되어 가사없이 전승되는 풍류음악의 대표적 기악곡이다.

Yeongsan hoesang 靈山會相佛菩薩 (Bound)*

Placing bamboo on the hole
Collecting breath in neatness
Piercing the bamboo pipe
Plucking and tuning the string
Drawing the bow with elegance
Regulating the mind with composure
Tapping the conscience with awareness
Treading carefully between sounds
Like the soft curve of a bamboo
Topped with a pointed mountain
Smooth yet clear
Graceful yet without excess
I hear the Buddha's words
Through my eyes and ears
Chanting in unison
Praising the compassion and virtue of Bodhisattva
At Ling Shan Mountain where the Lotus Sutra was taught.

---

* According to the "Akhak Gwebeom," a music record from the 5th century, Yeongsan Hoesang was originally a Buddhist music piece sung to the accompaniment of orchestral music with Buddhist lyrics about the Yeongsan Hoesang Bodhisattva. However, in modern times, it has become secularized and is now a representative instrumental piece of traditional Korean music, transmitted without lyrics.

너의 힘 (Strong)

너, 그렇게 소리를 지를 수 있는 사람이었어?
오장육부가 한 목소리로
목구멍이 시큼해지도록 용트름을 하더라
네가 하고 싶은 것이 그거였어?
그러려던 거였어?
이를 앙다물고 턱을 바닥까지 끌며 발을 구르더라
휘청거리지 않으려면 무게를 느껴야지
네가 느낀 만큼 땅이 메아리친다.
이게 네 무게라고
땅의 목소리가 근육을 타고 합창한다

땅에게 말해줘 네 무게를
땅에게 말해줘 네 의도를

Your strength (Strong)

You, were you someone who could raise your voice like that?

With one voice, belly made our throats sour

Was that what you wanted?

What you had planned all along?

Teeth clenched, chin to the ground, feet rolling

To stand firm, you must feel the weight

As much as you feel, the ground echoes

This is your weight

The voice of the earth echoes in unison with your muscles

Tell the earth your weight

Tell the earth your intention

미노타우로스의 연인 (light/rising)

그녀가 사뿐사뿐 걸어온다
예수가 물 위를 걸어 베드로에게 다가오듯
옷자락을 휘날리며
한숨이 땅을 꺼트리지 않게
살그머니 발끝을 들고
잠이 든 그의 무지한 얼굴에 볼을 비빈다

그만하라 이미 족하다

실반지처럼 금이 간 그녀의 갈비뼈와
푸르스름 멍든 그녀의 어깨
거칠게 움켜쥐었던 하얀 목덜미
상처가 중력처럼
악다귀처럼
불 끓는 지하로 끌어내리려 할 때
애증이 샴쌍둥이의 메아리처럼
계곡에서 되새김질 될 때

이 땅의 미로를 벗어나는 또 하나의 방법

팔을 높이 들고
그녀가 웅얼거린다
내 이웃을 내 몸과 같이 사랑하게 하옵소서

그만하라 이미 족하다

Lover of the Minotaur (light/rising)

She walks with a skip in her step
Jesus walks on water, approaching Peter
with fluttering clothes
Holding up her spindly legs
so that a sigh doesn't disturb the earth
I press my cheek against his ignorant face as he sleeps

Stop it, it's enough already.

Her ribs have a crack like thin ring
Her shoulders, a drowsy blue
The white nape of her neck, tightly gripped
The wounds like gravity
Like a devil's pitchfork
When it tries to drag her down to the seething
underworld
In the valley, like the echo of Siamese twins
Love-hate reverberates, resounding again

Another way to escape the maze of this earth

Lift your arms high

She roars

Make me love my neighbor like I love my own body

Stop it, it's enough already.

무수 (Indirect)

이 황량한 언덕에서 바람 소리를 들어봐
어디서부터 불어왔는지
어디로 가는지 알 수 없지만
절벽을 핥고 거친 골짜기를 할퀴는
어둠 속에선
보이지 않는 소리가 더 잘 들리고
우린 쉽게 겁에 질리지
모든 것을 헤아릴 순 없어
밤이 되면 한 치 앞이 안 보여도
하늘 가까운 귤빛 사구 위에서 별들을 봐야지
아! 반짝이는 것들과 어둠의 깊이를!

모든 것을 헤아릴 순 없어

Innumberable (indirect)

Listen to the sound of wind on this barren hill

We cannot tell where it came from

Nor where it will go

But in the darkness that grazes the cliffs

And scrapes the rugged valleys

Invisible sounds are heard clearer

We are easily frightened

We cannot comprehend everything

But at night, even if we cannot see beyond our noses

We must gaze at the stars on the orange-colored Milky
Way above

Ah! The sparkling things and the depth of darkness

We cannot comprehend everything

열망훈련 (Direct)

너에게 배웠다
무엇에 집중한다는 것을

화장실 문도 열어놓고 변기에 앉아
가늘고 긴 폭포수 소리를 반주로
너를 위해 노래를 부른다
잠시라도 눈에 보이지 않으면 죽을 것 같이
울며불며 어린 것이 기어 온다

우리가 이렇게 공부를 한다면 방방곡곡 서울대를 지어야지
우리가 이렇게 마음공부를 한다면 집집마다 사원을 지어야지

Aspiration training (Direct)

I learned from you
What it means to focus

Even leaving the bathroom door open and sitting on the toilet
With the sound of a narrow and long waterfall as the accompaniment
I sing a song for you
feel like you will die if you can't see me for even a moment
While crying, screaming, crawling like a child

If we study like this, we should build Harvard University in every nook and cranny
If we study the mind like this, we should build a shrine in every home

물고 있는 쥐 (Direct)

신식 여자들은 똑똑해서 멀티태스킹을 잘한다는데
나에겐 한도 초과
가물은 들녘에 내리는 비처럼 피곤이 얼룩진다
이 일과 저 일에 마음을 분주하게 리셋하니
번쩍번쩍 휴즈가 끊어진다
핸드폰 들고 핸드폰 찾고
냉장고 문 열고 한참을 서있는다
추리소설처럼 찾는 것은 가까이 있고
선거공약처럼 찾고자 했던 것은 쉽게 잊힌다
어디론가 달려 나가며 운전대를 잡고
빨래 삶는다고 얹어둔 들통 불
껐는지 안 껐는지 뜯어진 솔기같은 기억
나아가야 할 일과 당장 수습할 일이 맞선다

한 번에 한 가지만 하자
아버지가 말씀하셨지
물고 있는 쥐나 잘 물고 있으렴

The Mouse Holding Its Prey (Direct)

They say modern women are good at multitasking
But for me, it's too much to handle
Tiredness spreads like rain falling on a hazy field
Having to busily reset my mind between this task and
that,
The fuses keep blowing out in flashes
I find myself holding my phone while searching for my
phone
Standing in front of the fridge for a while
Like a detective, what I'm looking for is right in front of
me
Like election promises, What was sought after is easily
forgotten
I rush out, grab the steering wheel, and drive away
The fire for boiling laundry, placed upon the pot
Did I put it out or not Memories like torn seams
There's always something that needs to be done

Let's focus on one thing at a time
As my father once said,
Be like the mouse holding its prey

매직아이 (No space)

네 안에 있는 것들의 스탬프처럼
우리는 아는 것만 볼 수 있지
보려고 하는 것만 보지 말고
초점을 거두고 전체를 보렴
느슨한 눈동자가
진면목을 만난다

Magic eyes (No space)

As if the stamps of things inside of you,
We can only see what we know.
Don't just look at what you want to see,
Look at the whole picture while putting the focus aside
Loose pupils
meet the true nature

어느 완벽주의자의 사랑 (Sustained)

항상 미련이 남았다
할 수 있다면 좀 더!
너를 바라보고 싶었다

우리가 미처 가보지 못한
맛보지 못한
속삭이지 못한 모든 것들을 두고
한 발짝도 못 떼겠어

완성되지 않은 것들은 시간을 불러 세운다

The Love of a Perfectionist (Sustained)

I always had some regrets
If only I could do a little more!
I wanted to keep looking at you

For all the things we haven't tasted, seen
And whispered to each other,
I can't even take one step away

Unfinished things call for time

집시 여인 (Passion drive)

타오르는 모닥불 옆
붉은 드레스를 입은 눈 먼 여자가
굽슬거리는 머리를 묶고 춤을 춘다
그녀는 불꽃이었을 것이다
누구든 앞에 선 이를 집어삼키며
더욱 불타올랐을
사랑과 미움의 변이 만든 각처럼
뾰족한 혓바닥을 날름거리며
눈을 감고 기타 소리에 허밍 하며
지나온 일들을
용서하지 못한 것들에 대한
모자랐던 사랑을
쉰 목소리로 노래할 것이다
타오르다 타오르다 스스로 꺼져버릴
오래된 외로움으로 울 것이다

Gypsy Woman (Passion drive)

By the blazing bonfire

A blind woman in a red dress

Wraps up her tangled hair and dances

She would have been a flame

Burning even more

Anyone standing in front of her

Would have been swallowed up

Like the corners created by the twists of love and hate

Her pointed tongue flicks

Humming along with the guitar

She will sing about the things she has been through

The love that was not enough

And the things she cannot forgive

In a husky voice

She will cry with old loneliness

Burning, burning, and finally extinguishing herself

어느 4월 (Press)

어느 정치인이 세월호 이야기는 진저리난다고 했다
또 그 이야기를 들먹인다며
철없는 것들은 혀 짧은 소리를 한다

아이들이 숨을 멎은 그 날, 그 바다에서
어미들의 숨도 함께 멎었다
더 이상 바다에서 떠오르지 않게
심장을 묶고
겨울이 되면 뼈와 이가 시릴 것이다
그 차가운 물 속의 아이들처럼

농약을 먹고 목숨을 끊은 외삼촌의 뒷방에는
자신도 잊은 아기 같은 그의 어미가 있었다
어쩌면 그의 어미도 손으로 알았을 것이다
눈물처럼 떨어지는 이불의 꽃무늬를
하염없이 가위로 오려내며
아들을 보낸 슬픔을 대신했을 것이다

자식을 잃은 어미들은

그날이 되면 공명한다
애간장 끊는 고통으로
마리아 마리아를 부르며
아이들이 있는 마음의 해저
그 밑바닥으로 무겁게 가라앉는다
시간이 수중추처럼 그녀들을 끄당긴다

A certain April (Press)

A certain politician said that the story of the Sewol Ferry
disaster is tiresome
and mocked those who still talk about it
The tongue of the naive speaks shallowly

On the day when the children's breath was taken away in
that sea
their mothers' breath was taken away with them
Tying their hearts so that they would no longer emerge
from the sea
Their hearts will also freeze along with their bones and
teeth when winter comes
Like the children in the cold water.

the uncle who took his own life with pesticides stayed
In the beside room there was his mother
who had forgotten herself like a baby
Perhaps his mother also knew it with her hands
As tears fell like flower patterns on the quilt

She endlessly cut them off with scissors
Sympathizing with the grief of sending off her son

Mothers who have lost their children
echo with grief on that day
with the pain of cutting the red thread of destiny
they call out "Maria, Maria"
The bottom of their hearts, where their children are
sinks heavily to the sea floor
Time drags them down like a submerged anchor

기댈 수 없는 방 (State)

벽이 끊임없이 물러난다
기댈 수 없는 방이라니
내 등은 한없이 멀어지는 벽을 그리워한다
방 한가운데 의자에 앉은 노인이
꾸짖듯이 말하는 것 같다
그 방을 뛰쳐나가고 싶은데
악몽의 주인공들은 언제나 다리가 무감각하다
무한히 커지는 방에서
팝콘처럼 다다닥거리는 심장소리
벽 없는 방에서 문을 찾는다

Receding room (State)

The wall keeps receding

An unbearable room, it seems

My back longs for the wall now far away

In the center of the room, an old man sits

As if scolding me with his words

I want to flee this room

But the protagonist of the nightmare always has numb legs

In the infinitely expanding room

Heartbeats echo like popping corn

In a wall-less room searching for the door

3부 형태와 공간 속에서
IN SHAPE AND SPACE

미희언니 (Space)

그녀의 부모님은 화전민이었어
산기슭을 불태워 밭을 일구고
밤이 되면 흙집 단칸방 짚을 깔고
온 식구가 나란히 누웠지
깊은 밤 악몽이라도 꾸었을까 오줌을 싸면
돗자리 같이 엮은 짚더미가
산기슭에 번지는 불처럼 번져서
온 식구가 잠에서 깨어 일어났지
코끝이 빨갛게 시린 겨울
엄마의 따뜻한 옆구리를 굴처럼 파고들어
몸에 맞는 새 옷과 내 방을 원하던
여드름 덕지덕지 사춘기를 지나고
여전히 주인집 방 한 칸을 세 들어 사는 청춘
페인트칠이 다 벗겨진 삐걱이는
쥐구멍 같은 철문을 여닫으며
어쨌든 대학은 다녔네
졸업을 앞두고 참 변할 것이 없지만
모든 것이 불확실했던 여름날
유일하게 선명했던 것은 화투장뿐이었지

오줌을 참아가며

패를 탓하며

객들과 연신 담배를 태우기도 했던

너구리 굴을 나와

어느 날 홀연히 하나님 믿는 남자와 결혼했다지

가까이 있다고 모든 것이 가까운 것은 아니지만

가난을 깔고 자는 이들의 공간은

씨실과 날실처럼 엮여있어

예수님의 무덤도 굴이었다지

그 나라가 하늘에 임한 것처럼 땅에서도 이루어지옵소서, 아

멘

Sister Meehee (Space)

Her parents were farmers

They burned the mountainside to till the fields

At night, they laid down on a bed of straw in a small mud
hut

The whole family slept side by side

Did they have nightmares in the deep of the night as they
peed?

The straw mats, woven together like blankets,

spread like wildfire on the mountainside,

and the whole family woke up from their sleep

nose froze in the chilly winter,

burrowed into mother's warm side like a mole

After getting past the pimpled adolescence

when wanted new clothes and own room,

she was still living in a rent room

The old, squeaky iron door that has lost its paint

opens and closes like a mouse hole

Anyway, she did go to college

Nothing much has changed as graduation approaches,

but in the uncertain days of summer

the only clear line was the line of Oriental card deck

As she held her pee,

blaming her bad luck,

and smoking with the strangers who came by,

She emerged from the raccoon's den

and one day, she suddenly married a man who believed in
God

Just because things are close doesn't mean they're near

The space where the poor sleep is

woven together like a silkworm cocoon

I heard Jesus' tomb was a cave

May Your Kingdom come on earth as it is in heaven,
Amen.

쉐입 스크램블

advancing 어느 시인의 말처럼 '생은 때로 먼 길을 원한다'*

rising   나는 나 이상의 것을 원했지

spreading 나의 더 많은 부분이 너에게 닿고 싶었어

enclosing 모든 나그네들은 돌아갈 집을 꿈꾸지

sinking   빛들은 낮은 곳에도 임한다

retreating 얼마나 다행이야 물러나 바라볼 수 있어서

---

* 장석남의 '우리 집에 내려오는 양은 쟁반 하나' 중

Shape Scramble

advancing   Like a poet said, 'Life sometimes desires a long journey'

rising   I wanted something beyond myself

spreading   I wanted more of me to reach you

enclosing   All wanderers dream of their home to return

sinking   The light shines even in low places

retreating   How fortunate I'm to be able to step back and look at it

삼 년 고개*

어느 겨울 산 장비 없이 올랐다가
도토리처럼 굴러 내려온 적이 있다
삼 년 고개를 굴러 내려온 노인마냥
나는 아직도 굴러떨어지고 있었다
알고 있지?
구를 땐 한없이 작아져야 한단다
가장 낮은 곳에 도착하여서야 비로서
깔깔깔깔 거칠게 웃을 수 있게 된 것을 기뻐하며
매번 새로이 너를 만날 수 있는 것을 기뻐하며
아집의 관객이 된 것을 기뻐하며
딛고 일어서야지
까치발을 들고 멀리 보이는 너에게
손을 흔들어야지

---

* 한국의 전래동화 중에 넘어지면 삼 년 만 사는 고개에 대한 이야기가 있다. 어느 날
한 노인이 삼 년 고개에서 넘어져서 삼 년 만 살게 될 것을 염려하자 손자가 삼 년 고
개에서 굴러내려오면 오래 살게 될 것이라고 해결해 준다.

On the Three-Year Hill*

Once I climbed a mountain in winter without any gear
And rolled down like an acorn
Like an old man who rolled down Three-Year Hill
I was still tumbling down
Do you know?
When rolling, you should become infinitely smaller
Only when you arrive at the lowest point
Delighted to be able to laugh coarsely and loudly
Be happy to be able to meet you anew every time
Be happy to become a spectator of arrogance
Get up and stand
Holding magpie feet
waving my hand to you in the distance

---

* There is a Korean folk tale about the "Three-Year Hill," where if someone
falls, they will only live for three more years. One day, an old man falls on the
hill and worries that he will only live for three more years. His grandson assures
him that if he rolls down the hill, he will live a long life.

적당한 거리

가까이 다가오는 순간
뒷걸음치며 거리를 둔다
뻣뻣한 목 위에 굳은 얼굴을 얹은 채로
상처는 소스라치게 재생되고
현재는 차갑게 얼어붙는다
폭력은 재규어처럼
덮치고 물어뜯고 집어삼킨다
돌아설 수 없는
끝낼 수 없는 만찬의 밤

놀라지 않는 용감한 심장을 원했던 사자처럼
스스로 힘을 알아차리기까지
밤은 긴장되고 모든 걸음은 조심스러웠다
목덜미의 갈기를 부드럽게 날리며
그의 눈을 담담히 주시하리
너도 사자의 살점을
뜯어 삼킬 수는 없겠지

빛과 어둠이
내 얼굴의 수 천 각도로 스며든다

Profer distance

When approaching too closely
I step back, keeping a distance
My stiff neck with a hardened face
The wounds reopen, the present freezes
Violence attacks like a jaguar
Pouncing, tearing, devouring
A never-ending banquet I can't escape

Like a lion seeking a brave, unflinching heart
Until I recognize my own strength
The night is tense, every step cautious
Gently fluttering the mane at the nape of the neck
I calmly gaze into its eyes
You can't tear and devour
The lion's flesh, can you?

Light and darkness
Pervade my face from countless angles.

플레이팅

엄마를 모시고 고급레스토랑에 가서
누군가의 일당을 1인분으로 지급하고
매 끼니 그런 음식만 먹는척하며
입에 척척 음식을 붙인다

묵직하고 두꺼운 접시에
파운데이션처럼 얇게 펴 바른 소스 위에
먹을 수도 없는 파슬리 조각과
가녀린 수삼이 굽이치는 산등성이처럼
드러누워 있다

속옷 서랍에 넘치게 쟁여둔 보풀 난 양말처럼
가로세로 빡빡한 일정 말고
월급보다 긴 카드 명세서 같은 작업 목록 말고

고급이란 시공을 허락하는 것
수삼의 잔뿌리 한 올 한 올
모두 드러내도 좋다고
이 모든 공간을

너를 위해 비워두어도 좋다고
수삼 혼자 여여한 접시를 앞에 두고
대자로 온몸을 열고 그렇게 눕고 싶다

Plating

I go to a fancy restaurant with my mother,
pretend to pay for someone else's meal,
and stick food to my mouth,
acting like I only eat that kind of food.

On a solid and thick plate,
thinly spread foundation-like sauce,
lays a piece of parsley that is impossible to eat,
and a thin slice of young roots of ginseng
that twists like a mountain path.

like a woolen sock full of lint in my underwear drawer,
not with a tight schedule
or a credit card statement longer than my paycheck.

Luxury is allowing for time and space
to lay out each strand of ginseng root,
to clear out all the space,
even if it means a lonely plate of ginseng,

and to lay down on the table
with arms and legs wide open

꿈

어느 밤 꿈을 꾸었다
닌자 차림의 정자들이 일제히 난자를 만나러 달려갔다
정자들은 갈림길에서 망설임 없이 날렵하게 길을 선택했다
한쪽은 아무것도 없을 텐데
저렇게 헛되이 맹렬하구나
난자를 만나지 못할 정자들이 안되었다 생각했다
그런 생각이 들켰는지
아무것도 없는 길 끝에서
숨을 헐떡이며 정자가 말한다
우린 한 팀이야
우리 중 하나는 난자를 만나고
우리는 그의 훌륭한 페이스 러너가 되어준 거지
무언가 잉태된다는 것은 그런 거야
커다란 반죽기계가 작동하고
많은 것들이 반죽 입구로 행진하였다
반죽이 나온 입구에 완두콩이 쏟아졌다
완두콩 콩깍지를 열어보니
초록색 실한 콩알이 나란히 누워있다
그리고, 맨 끝 쪼글쪼글하고 납작한 콩알과

콩알을 꿈꾸는 작은 연두색 덩어리가 있었다
나는 이것들을 심으면 싹이 날까 걱정했다
그러자 곧 반죽기계 입구에서
다리가 세 개인 하얀 송아지가 나왔고
인도사람이 다가와
이마에 빨간 틸락(tilak)을 그려주며
기도를 하자 여신이 되었다
우리는 꽃을 뿌리며 춤을 추었다
그리고 반죽기계로 다시 걸어 들어갔다

Dream

One night, I had a dream.

Ninjas dressed as sperm rushed to meet the egg.

The sperm decisively chose their path at the crossroads.

I thought, 'One path will lead to nothing.

What a waste of effort.'

I feel sorry for all sperms not reaching the egg.

Perhaps sensing my doubt,

a sperm at the end of the empty path

gasped and said,

"We're a team.

One of us will reach the egg,

and the rest of us will be his excellent pacemakers.

This is how things are conceived."

A giant mixing machine began to operate,

and many things marched toward the opening.

When the dough emerged,

soybeans spilled out of the opening.

Inside the green pods were rows of plump green beans.

And at the end,

there were small, bumpy, flat beans,

and a small, green lump dreaming of becoming a bean.

I was worried that if I planted them, they wouldn't grow.

Then, a white calf with three legs appeared from the
dough,

and a Hindu priest approached,

Drawing a red tilak on it's forehead

and praying, It became a goddess.

We scattered flowers and danced,

and then walked back into the mixing machine.

떠나는 자들 (Back)

뒤를 돌아보지 마요
롯의 아내처럼 소금기둥이 되지 않도록
붙잡고 싶고
되돌리고 싶은 것들을 뒤로하고
화염을 뒤집어쓴 소돔과 고모라가
그저 불타오르도록
검게 사그라드는 마음의 도시를 떠나요
눕고 싶고
먹고 싶고
탐하고 싶은
욕망의 도시에서
잠 못 들고
미각을 잃고
사랑하는 법을 잊어버린
무력하게 기울어지는 옛 몸은 남겨두고
미처 짐을 챙기지 못해 차라리 홀가분해진 그대로

떠나는 자들이여
뒤를 돌아보지 마요

Departing Ones (Back)

Do not look back
Like Lot's wife, lest you become a pillar of salt
Leave behind what you want to hold on to
And let Sodom and Gomorrah,
with flames inverted,
Just burn and crumble away
Leave the city of your heart that withers to ash
In the city of desire,
where you want to lie down,
Eat
and coveted
sleepless,
And losing taste
Forgetful of love,
Leaving behind the old body that leans helplessly
In fact, it's more comfortable
not having managed to pack up just as it is

Departing ones,
Do not look back.

쥐불놀이(Transform)*

움직이는 것들은 흔적을 남겨

말들에 대한 기억도 길이 있는지

녹음해 둔 테잎을 뇌 어딘가에 심어둔 양

내가 말한 적이 있었던가

언젠가 너를 붙잡고 똑같은 이야기를 한 적이 있지

네가 너를 설명하는 그 방식으로

매번 행동을 정당화하려는 것을 느낄 때처럼 찜찜하다

너의 궤도는 잘 보이는데

이 생각과 저 생각 사이

바늘귀에 실을 달고 오가며

옴짝달싹 못하게 궤도를 홀친다

쥐불놀이의 밤

논두렁의 쥐들은 위태롭다

빛이 궤도를 만들며 춤을 출 때

새로운 길로 궤도의 축을 옮길 때

---

* 쥐불놀이는 정월대보름 전날에 논둑이나 밭둑에 불을 지르고 돌아다니며 노는 한국 전통 민속놀이 중 하나이다. 깡통에 구멍을 내어 짚단 등을 넣고 불을 붙여 빙빙돌리다가 던져 잡초를 태우고 해충이나 쥐의 피해를 줄이고자 실시되었다. 상징적으로 액운과 재앙을 태워준다는 뜻이 있고 쥐불의 크고 작음에 따라 그 해의 풍흉을 점치기도 한다.

나를 이야기하는 방식에서 놓여날 때
600만 가지의 새로운 궤도에서
들판 사방이 환해진다

Playing with Fireflies (Transform)*

Moving things leave traces

Is there a length to the memory of horses?

Like planting a recorded tape somewhere in the brain,

Have I ever told you the same story before?

It feels uneasy, like your constant justification of actions

In the way you describe yourself

Your orbit is clearly visible

but between this thought and that

going back and forth like threading a needle with a string

I disturb the orbit so that it can't move smoothly

On a night of playing with fireflies

The mice in the rice fields are precarious

When the light makes a dance on the orbit

---

* Jwibulnori is one of the traditional Korean folk games played on the eve of Jeongwol Daeboreum, the first full moon of the lunar year. People would light fires and roam around rice paddies and field embankments. They would make holes in tin cans, insert straw or twigs, and light them on fire. The flaming cans would then be spun around and thrown to burn weeds, aiming to reduce damage from pests and rodents. Symbolically, Jwibulnori is believed to burn away bad luck and disasters. The size of the fire is also used to predict the fortune and misfortune of the year.

When the axis of the orbit is shifted to a new path

When I am revealed in a different way of storytelling

The surroundings become bright with 6 million new orbits

에고

아가를 보듬는 그녀의 손길 한 줌
기저귀를 갈며 부채질해주던 바람 한 줌
미음을 입에 넣어주며 웃던 미소 한 줌
눈에 넣을 듯 바라보던 눈길 한 줌
너무 질지 않게
너무 되지 않게
말랑말랑하게 반죽하여
형상을 만들어 생기를 불어 넣는다

엄마를 언제든 불러올 수 있는 작은 창작

Ego

A handful of her touch that used to soothe a baby
A handful of wind that used to fan the diaper change
A handful of smile that used to feed the porridge
A handful of gaze that used to cherish the moment

Softening and molding the shape
Not too rough
Not too polished
Bringing life to the dough

A small creation that calls for mom, anytime

느린 학습자

암세포도 생명이잖아요 같이 지내보려고요

잘생긴 드라마 남자 주인공은
숙연히 무리수 대사를 읊었지만
난 작은 가위를 배꼽에 넣고 싹둑 잘라냈다

발병 전, 세포들은 때가 되면 사라졌겠지만
죽어야 할 세포가 증식했더라도
무심함에 미생(未生)으로 말라 비틀어졌을 거다

그 놈이 부드럽고 축축한 내 몸에 뿌리를 내리자
극심히 피곤하고 잠을 못 자는 증상들이
고성제를 가르쳐 주었다

어쩌면 그 놈이 중기, 말기를 거쳐 완생(完生)하면서
집착이 이 모든 고통의 원인이고
이것을 멸하는 방법과 도에 이르는 방법을 알았을까

입과 머리가 안 것을

몸으로 옮겨 심어
암세포 마냥 증식할 수 있다면
정상이 아닐까

배움이 더디다

The Slow Learner

Even cancer cells are a form of life, let's try living together

The handsome actor lead of a drama
Uttered lines far beyond his abilities
But I just cut them out with small scissors

Before the onset, the cells would have disappeared in due
time
Even if the dying cells had proliferated
They would have withered away, turning into nothingness
due to neglect

As it rooted itself in my soft and moist body
Severe symptoms of fatigue and insomnia taught me
The Truth of Suffering

Perhaps if it had survived through intermediate and
advanced stages
And attained enlightenment and the way to eliminate

attachment

It could have known the cause of all this pain

If I could transfer the emptiness of my mouth and mind
Into my body and let it proliferate like cancer cells
Wouldn't it be a sign of abnormality?

Learning is slow

손으로 보는 법 (Touch)

눈은 마음의 창이라고 했는데
점점 뿌연해진다
눈알이 울뚝불뚝 경련이 오는 듯 불편하다
눈물을 적당히 머금고 살아야 했건만
마음의 둑방이 무너지고
온몸의 물들은 범람하니
햇볕이 쨍하면 건조해지기 마련이다
눈을 감으면 미처 읽지 못한
마음의 땅이 쩍쩍 갈라지는 소리가 들린다

항상 의외의 것을 떠올리는 상상력 풍부한 도반 한 명이
최근 녹내장으로 시력을 잃을 위기란다
그녀가 책을 너무 많이 보긴 했다
평생 읽을 책을 너무 빨리 읽어버렸는지도 모른다
그럴 줄 알고 그녀는 미리 손으로 읽는 법을 배웠다
사람이라는 책을 손으로 읽다 보면
눈이 읽지 못한 것을 알게 될 터이다

마음의 땅이 갈라진 틈새를 어루만지며
눈먼 이 점자책 읽듯
관세음보살처럼
세상의 소리를 볼 것이다

The way of seeing with hands (Touch)

They say eyes are the windows to the soul
But they're getting blurry day by day
My eyes twitch and convulse uncomfortably
As if they're plagued with seizure
I was supposed to hold back my tears and live on
But my emotional dam crumbled
and my whole being was flooded
When the sun shines too brightly, I become parched
Closing my eyes, I hear the sound of my heartland
cracking

The imaginative and erudite Da Vinci
Is now at risk of losing her sight to glaucoma
Maybe she read too many books in her lifetime
And read them too quickly, I suppose
That's why she learned to read with her hands
By reading people like a book with her hands
She'll discover things her eyes couldn't see
Like running her fingers over the cracks in her heartland

Like reading a blind man's braille book

Like the bodhisattva Guan Yin

She will see the world's sound through touch

기면

어쩌면 우리는 잠들기 위해서 살고 있는지도 몰라요
영원에 접속하는 그 순간을 알아차리고 기뻐하기 위해
밥을 먹고
일을 하고
노래를 하죠
삶의 한낮은 기운 배의 반대쪽 수심을 헤아리느라
이토록 분주한가 봐요

모든 인생이 그렇듯 영원한 잠에 이르기까지
틈틈이 잠들며
산맥으로 떠오른 해저와
가라앉는 섬들의 시간을 알아차려요
모든 일을 파할 때가 되면 길을 나서듯
배가 기울면 바다에 빠지듯
얼굴을 씻고 기도를 하듯이 손을 모으고 누워
그 순간을 알아차려요

Narcolepsy

Perhaps we are living to fall asleep

To recognize and be happy that moment of eternal connection

we eat

and work

and sing

The midday of life is so busy

Measuring the depth of the opposite side of the tilted boat

Like all lives, until we reach the eternal sleep

We occasionally fall asleep, realizing the time

Of mountain ranges rising from the sea and

Of islands sinking into it

When it's time to complete everything like setting out on a journey

Like falling into the sea when the boat tilts,

Washing my face and laying down with my hands together

recognize that moment

오유지족 (吾唯知足)

살아서 영생을 누리겠다는 어머니
그 고난의 십자가를 진 예수도
죽은 자 가운데 살아나셨다니
기적이란 믿는 자만의 징표 아니겠어요
병들지도 않고
가난도 없고
죽음도 없다니
수지도 이런 수지가 없는데
당신에게 보이는 것이 내게는 보이지 않으니
목침 대신 내 팔을 베고 누우세요
앙상하게 가죽만 남은 볼에 입 맞추고
그 입에 뜨신 밥을 여미고
그 손을 잡아 주름을 펴고
아기처럼 기저귀를 갈아 드릴 테요
나에게 삶이란
늘 작아지고 사라지는 행보이니
한 이불 덮고 차가워진 어미 발을 부비며
우리에게 남은 온기에 감사할 테요
나에게 보이는 것이 당신에게 보이지 않으니

I only know contentment

My mother who wants to live forever
Even Jesus who carried the cross of suffering
Rose from the dead among the dead
Aren't miracles the signs only for those who believe?
No sickness
No poverty
There's no gain like this, where there's no gain at all
Instead of a pillow, rest on my arms
Gently kiss the cheek with only the skin left
Feed with the food in your mouth
Hold your hand, smooth out the wrinkles
I will change your diaper like a baby
Life to me is always a small and disappearing step
Covering you with a blanket, blowing on your cold feet
I will be grateful for the warmth that remains with us
Since what I see doesn't seem to be what you see

어떤 고타마에게 보내는 편지

당신의 고귀하신 생각은
굉장히 독특한 생각이고
다른 사람들이 이를 함부로 사용하여
불법적인 이득을 취할 것이
심히 염려되오니
필히 저작권 등록하여 주시고
당신의 깨달음에 대해
정해진 사원에서 가르침 받지 못한
모든 이의 알아차림이나
포교활동을 금해주시기를 요청드립니다.

자본주의 지식회사 대표

A Letter to a Great Tathagata

Your noble thoughts
are very unique,
and I am deeply concerned that others
may use them recklessly for illegal gain.
Therefore, please register your copyright and request
that your teachings not be used for commercial purposes
or missionary activities by those who
have not received proper training at designated temples.

Sincerely,
CEO of the Capitalist Knowledge Company

얘는 잘 몰라

어느 깊은 밤 세포들이 웅성이는 소리가 들렸다
얘는 잘 몰라
40조 세포들이 모여 심장되고, 내장되어 말하는 소리도
얘는 잘 몰라
우리가 어디서 왔고 어디로 가는지도
얘는 잘 몰라
우리의 소리를 가만히 듣는 관찰자도
얘는 잘 몰라
우리가 왜 이렇게 모여서 육체의 사원을 짓는지도
얘는 잘 몰라
우리가 지은 사원을 허물며 기쁘게 춤추는 순간도
얘는 잘 몰라
땅 속의 눈 먼 곤충들이 우리를 나누어 품는 이유도
얘는 잘 몰라
어느 산 속 달그림자에 놀라 한참을 웅크리고 있는 걸
얘는 잘 몰라

얘! 눈 떠!

She doesn't know

On a deep night, I heard the sound of cells murmuring

But she doesn't know

That 40 trillion cells come together to form the heart and

organs, and speak

She doesn't know

Where we came from or where we're going

She doesn't know

About the observer who quietly listens to our sounds

She doesn't know

Why we gather like this to build the temple of flesh

She doesn't know

About the moment we joyfully dance while tearing down

the temple we built

She doesn't know

The reason why blind insects in the ground embrace us

She doesn't know

About the moment she crouches in surprise in the shadow

of a mountain

She doesn't know

Hey, wake up!

집 앞으로 돌아오는 방법 (Pre-Axis)

2월의 어느 날
봄이 오고 있다
설렘이 아지랑이처럼 피어오르고
아직 아무것도 시작되지 않는 두근거림
그냥 나로 있을 수 있는 편안함 속에서
아이는 집을 멀리 떠나보고 싶다
그래 멀리 나가 보자꾸나
자꾸자꾸 걸어 나가 보자꾸나
이 골목을 나가 다음 골목을 선택할 수 있다는 것은
정처 없고 즐거운 심사이다

그 고비 끝에 귀향한 알라딘이
또 짐을 싸서 나서듯이
가보지 않았던 골목길을 기웃거리며
막다른 길을 돌아 나오며
아까 왔던 길이라 킥킥거리며
아주 멀리 집 앞을 걸어 돌아올 것이다.

Returning to one's doorstep (Pre-Axis)

On a certain day in February
Spring is coming
Excitement blooms like a rash
The anticipation of things yet to start
In the comfort of being able to just be myself
My daugther wants to leave home and go far away
Yes, let's go far away and see
Let's keep on walking and walking
Choosing the next alley outside of this one
Is an exciting and directionless prospect

Like Aladdin, returning home after his ordeal
Only to pack bags and set off again
She wanders through unexplored alleys
And turns around at dead ends
Kicking the ground, grumbling about the road he just
came from
She will eventually walk all the way back home.

실현 (Matching Touch)

몸을 읽는 법을 배우며
알게 되었다.
내가 만나러 가는 방식으로
그도 만나러 온다

"너, 모르는 소리야
무턱대고 어떻게 사람을 믿어
눈뜨고 코 베는 세상에
순진한 소리 해 댄다."
모든 놈들이 뒤통수치고 떠나갈 놈들이었던
그녀의 믿음대로
모든 이들은 떠나갔다

그것 봐! 내가 뭐랬어!

Come true (Matching Touch)

As I learned to read my body
I realized that he, too, comes to meet me
In the same way I go to meet him

"You, it's all nonsense
How can you trust people without thinking?
You talk naively
In a world with open eyes and stinging noses."
But as she believed
Those who were all supposed to leave, did.

See, I told you!

노인의 담요

아이들은 일제히 절벽에서 뛰어내렸다
우는 아이를 달래는 인내심이
일자리를 잃은 청년들의 통장 잔고처럼
바닥을 드러낸 시대에 당연한 일이다
아이를 들쳐업고 몸으로 달래던 시대를 지나
울지 말고 말하라고 다그치는
입으로 거처를 옮긴 후
아이를 키우는 일은 주시하는 일이 되었다

가난한 자는 복이 있다는데
가난이란 원래 신경 쓸 일들이 많은 것이다
빈 젖 물은 아가의 빽빽거리는 울음을 달래듯
가파른 계단에서 노쇠만큼 허리를 바스러트리는
가난이란 원래 짊어질 짐이 많은 것이다

땅을 딛고 서있기 어려운 이들만이 남아
십자가에서 내려진 예수처럼
휘고 구부러진 허리를

뻣뻣하고 주름진 장막으로 감싸 안고
새끼손가락을 맞걸어 기도한다
노령의 기도처에서 우는 아이를 몸으로 안는다

The Old Man's Blanket

Children all jumped off the cliff together

Comforting a crying child with patience

is as common as the bank balance of the unemployed
youth

in an era where everything is laid bare

After the era of carrying and comforting children with
one's body has passed

raising a child has become a watchful task

telling them not to cry but to speak up

moving from one place to another through their mouths

It is said that the poor are blessed

for poverty naturally comes with many things to worry
about

As if soothing a wailing child, clinging to a milkless breast

On the steep stairs, bending backs as aged as time

poverty naturally comes with a heavy load to carry

Only those who find it difficult to stand on the ground remain
like Jesus descended from the cross
They hold their twisted, bending waists
Wrapped in a stiff and creased curtain
They cross their little fingers in prayer
In the prayer house of senescence embracing the weeping child

앉은뱅이 학자

어째 똑바로 서 있을 수가 없당께
무슨 공부를 그 나이 먹도록 뭣허고 허냐
해도 해도 끝이 없는 게 인생 공분디
벌이도 시원찮은 것이
어찌 그리 주머니 털어가며
개털이 됨시롱
그리 배우러 댕긴다고 허냐

오메 된그 어쯔까잉
고기 낚는 법을 배우라니께
음메 고래사냥 하는 법까지 배워 뿌러라
수 천 수 만 가지 다 배워서
산으로 병풍 두른 이 산골짜기에서
뭘 낚으려고 하는겐지

그 책 보따리 일단 내려놓고
서 봐!
서 있을 수는 있는겨?

Armchair scholar

Ah cain't seem ta stan' up straight,

What's th' point o' studyin' so hard at that age?

Life's bitter feud is that there's no end ta it,

Even th' hard-earned money is nothin' much.

How kin folks spend money so frivolously,

An' end up with jus' a few pennies left?

What's th' use o' learnin' how ta fish,

Or even how ta hunt whales?

Learnin' thousands upon thousands o' things,

Jus' ta catch somethin' in this here remote mountain valley.

Put down that stack o' books,

An' stan' up!

Kin ya even stan'?

런던의 밤

다울랜드의 눈물의 파반느를 듣다가
문득 런던의 후미진 뒷골목 작은 방이 생각났다
그 시절은 떠나지 못하는 태양의 편지를
밤새 읽어야 하는 여름이었다
차라리 밤이 어서 오기를 바랬지만
칠흑 같은 어둠은 오지 않았다
아주 먼 여행을 마치고 당도한 파리한 빛이
나의 얼굴을 어루만졌다
그가 지켜보는 밤은
푸른 빛으로 가득 찼다
나는 먼지 같은 영혼을
텅 빈 침대 위에 모아
흩어지지 않도록 침묵했다

On a night in London

While listening to Daulland's Tears of Pavanne

I suddenly reminded of a small room in a back alley of London.

At that time, it was a summer where I had to stay up all night

To read the letter from the sun that couldn't leave me.

I hoped the night would come soon,

But the dark soil-like darkness didn't come.

Instead, the saturated light of Paris after a long journey

Caressed my face.

The night he watches over

is filled with pale blue light,

And I silently kept my dusty soul

Gathered on the empty bed

So that it wouldn't scatter.

유물론자의 마음

나라는 것의 현상
위태로운 개미탑처럼
단단하게 여물었다 한들
조각조각 부서진다

다른 이의 돈으로 맛있는 것을 사 먹으라는
인도의 옛 사상가처럼 말하지는 않을 테다
누군가를 울리고 소리치게 만드는 것은 딱 질색인데
그것이 기쁨인 자라면 말리지 않을 테다

나 자신으로 더 오래 머물기 위해*
영혼보다 더 좋은 마차는 없을 터인데

나에게 영적인 것이란
비튜겐슈타인의 방석에 앉아
헤아릴 수 없는 것들을
영원하지 않는 것들을

---

* 일본 애니메이션 「공각기동대」의 주제곡 가사 중

154

물끄러미 바라보는 것
날카로운 손톱을 바위로 짓이겨
소망이 부서진 마음들을
부드럽게 어루만지고 싶은
곰의 마음이다

이제 더 이상 내가 아니어도 좋겠다고 생각하는
나의 얇은 망사 같은 의식의 층
나는 천박한 때로 소박한 유물론자이다

The Mind of an Artifact Theorist

The phenomenon of self,
even if it is firmly carved like a shaky ant tower,
it breaks apart piece by piece.

I won't tell you to eat well with someone else's money,
like an old Indian Philosopher of materialism
that makes people cry and scream is just repulsive
But if that's someone's joy,
I won't stop them.

There is no better carriage than the soul,
to stay with myself longer.

To me, the spiritual is
to sit on Wittgenstein's chair
and gaze at
the immeasurable and
the impermanent things,
to soothe shattered hopes

with gentle claws
like a bear's heart.

My thin mesh of consciousness
that I now think is no longer me,
I'm just a vulgar or humble artifact theorist.

부모가 된다는 것

지상으로 착륙하다
절름발이가 된 신들이
어머니와 아버지가 된다
나의 어머니는 평생을 지상으로 내려오지 않는
하나님 아버지를 그리워하였고
나는 그 편이 더 나을 수도 있겠다 생각했다
절름발이가 된 신들은
아무것도 기억해내지 못하기 일쑤였고
어미가 되어 어미의 기억을
아비가 되어 아비의 기억을
대를 이어 되살리려 하지만
업이란 가물가물한 기억들의 전수이다

Becoming Parents

Landing on earth

Are gods with muted footsteps

Who become mothers and fathers

My mother longed for GOD who never descended

To earth throughout her life

And I thought that might be better

The gods with muted footsteps

Were unable to remember anything

But as mothers, they try to recall

Their own mothers' memories

As fathers, they try to recall

Their own fathers' memories

But memories passed down

In a hazy and ambiguous manner are Karma.

몸의 사원

발행일 | 2023년 8월 3일

지은이 | 이정미
책표지 | 박여원
펴낸이 | 마형민
편 집 | 신건희
펴낸곳 | (주)페스트북
주 소 | 경기도 안양시 안양판교로 20
홈페이지 | festbook.co.kr

ISBN 979-11-6929-323-5 03810
값 15,000원